The Girl
With A Donkey Tail
by Anne Rockwell

E. P. Dutton   New York

Copyright © 1979 by Anne Rockwell

Library of Congress Cataloging in Publication Data

Rockwell, Anne F. ` The girl with a donkey tail.

SUMMARY: The girl with a donkey tail embarks
on an arduous journey to find the princess who is
the rightful owner of a gold ring she found.
[1. Fairy tales] I. Title.
PZ8.R616Gi [E] 78-12823 ISBN 0-525-30661-7

Published in the United States by E. P. Dutton, a Division
of Sequoia-Elsevier Publishing Company, Inc., New York

Published simultaneously in Canada by Clarke,
Irwin & Company Limited, Toronto and Vancouver

Editor: Ann Durell   Designer: Riki Levinson

Printed in the U.S.A.   First Edition
10 9 8 7 6 5 4 3 2 1

for
Hannah, Elizabeth
and
Oliver

Chapter One

ONCE UPON A TIME, there was a little girl who lived in a cave with three bears. The bears could not talk, but they would growl and grunt pleasantly to the little girl, and they always shared their honey with her.

In return for their hospitality, she swept the cave with a broom made of dry tree branches and kept everything neat and tidy for them. Being bears, they were clumsy at things like housekeeping.

The little girl was quite content, except during the

long winter when the bears went into a deep and long-lasting sleep. Then she was lonely.

While the bears slept, cold winds blew and the snow lay outside bright and white. Inside the cave, it was dim and shadowy, but snug. To keep from growing too lonely, she would sing songs and tell stories she made up herself.

This little girl had a name, although the bears could not call her by it. It was Cloralinda. She knew this, or believed she did, from a dream she often had about herself.

In the dream she was moving slowly across acorns and mosses, mushrooms, moldy leaves and green ferns, while someone called from behind the trees, "Cloralinda, Cloralinda, Cloralinda. . . ." She never could see the person who called her. Then the calling would grow faint and faraway, and she would wake up. Awake, the dream became the story she knew best. But although the story had a middle, it had no beginning and no end.

Cloralinda had, besides her name, a tail like a donkey. She was an ordinary but pretty little girl in all other respects.

One morning, after an especially long winter, the bears stretched their big furry arms slowly in their sleep. Cloralinda looked out of the cave. Islands of snow lay in the forest, dripping and dirty. A muddy, wet smell mixed with growing green filled the air. The sun was shining and the trees dripped noisily. Their bark was wet and shining. Spring was coming.

Cloralinda knew that it was time to clean the cave so it would look especially nice when the bears woke up. Then they would be jolly and cheerful, and glad to see her. So she began to sweep in every dark corner and along the cave walls. She swept and swept until her arms were tired, and there was a big dusty heap near the opening into the forest.

A sudden sunbeam hit the pile of dust. Among the dead leaves, brown bear fur, bee wings, and spider webs, something shone back at the sunbeam. Cloralinda bent down and saw a little gold ring with one blood-red ruby. Inside the ring, in tiny but elegant script, was engraved:

Take me to the princess.

"And that is exactly what I must do," said Cloralinda to herself. She slipped the ring on her left hand for safe-keeping. Then, one by one, she kissed each big bear on its black and shiny nose and whispered, "Good-bye."

The bears stretched and grunted softly, but still they slept on.

Off went Cloralinda. She passed all the trees she knew so well: the oldest oak, the widest beech, the tallest pine, and the whitest birch. She stepped across the mossy stones in the brook where the ice was crackling loudly as it melted. She walked off into a dark part of the forest where she had never been before.

It was only as the sun went down and darkness began to come, that Cloralinda realized she had no idea who or where the princess was, and in what direction she should go.

Chapter Two

CLORALINDA WALKED DEEPER and deeper into the forest. She had no choice, for wherever she turned the trees grew tall and dark. Now all of them were pines. There was no snow, no ice, no leaves, no spring flowers, only mountains of pine needles that were prickly and soft.

In the darkness, she turned the little ring to make sure it was still on her hand. "How," she wondered sadly, "will I find the way to the princess, if indeed there is a way at all?"

5

And Cloralinda began to cry. This was most unusual, for she was as brave as she was neat and tidy. As she cried she grew very cold; first chilly, then she turned icy cold and trembling. As her teeth began to chatter, she was extremely surprised to hear a voice, although whether it was a voice or a song or a growl, she was not quite sure. She dried her tears with the tip of her tail and listened carefully.

"The pine needles are warm and dry."

Then the voice was silent. Cloralinda lay down in the pine needles and it was true, they were very warm and dry. She covered herself up cozily. She looked up to where she knew the sky must be, and searched for the moon or a familiar star. But she saw nothing at all, only the blackest blackness she had ever known. Then suddenly, she saw two bright red lights. They were quite close together and they glowed steadily.

"Such strange stars!" she thought sleepily and shut her eyes. But slowly she lifted her lids again and then she was *very* frightened. For the two red lights were not stars, but two red eyes of a living beast.

"But I must not cry," thought Cloralinda to herself, "for then whatever it is will surely eat me up," and she sniffed back a tear. She dared not move, and her toes began to tingle and grow numb.

Then a voice spoke. It sounded something like a song and something like a growl.

"Little girl, don't be afraid of me. Wiggle your toes and make yourself comfortable. Then go to sleep. You have come far, but you have much farther to go. Tomorrow I will show you the path out of my forest."

Then the beast sang Cloralinda to sleep.

Chapter Three

WHEN CLORALINDA WOKE, the forest was lit by a very dim morning light. Beside her stood a great gray wolf.

"Good morning," said the wolf, "I did not introduce myself properly last night. My name is Franz Lupus, and this is my part of the forest. Here all creatures can speak to one another in the language each understands best. When you leave my forest that will not be so. Bears will grunt as bears do, owls will hoot, geese will honk, ducks will quack, and foxes will yip."

Then Franz Lupus led Cloralinda to a spring where she drank, and a place where she ate pine nuts from the pinecones that littered the ground.

When she had eaten, the big wolf said, "Follow me." His paws padded swiftly and softly over the pine needles. Cloralinda ran after him. Then, suddenly, he stopped.

"I know who you are, and I know why you have come. You are right to take the ring to the princess, and you are brave to try. I can give you some help. Around my neck, you will find a rope which is tied with a strong knot, and on that rope there is a little pouch. Untie the knot."

And Cloralinda did, although it was indeed strong and hurt her hands. But at last she held the rope and she could see the little pouch.

"Inside that is a map," said Franz Lupus. "It will show you the shortest and safest route to the princess. But under no circumstances may you open the pouch until you are out of my forest. Use the rope to tie up your donkey tail. There is someone in this forest who would tweak your tail and play tricks on you. Watch out for him."

Cloralinda carefully tied up her tail with the rope that held the little pouch.

Then Franz Lupus said, "Tell me now, how will you know when you have left my forest?"

Cloralinda answered, "Bears will grunt as bears do,

owls will hoot, geese will honk, ducks will quack, and foxes will yip. No creature will be able to speak as I do."

"All that is true," said Franz Lupus. "And wolves may also bite, and you will come to a place where little girls have no donkey tails, and there you will find the princess. Now, look down at your feet."

Cloralinda did. There was one small pebble that was strangely bright. It looked like a tiny moon. "How beautiful!" said Cloralinda, and she reached for the pebble.

"Do not touch that!" said Franz Lupus sternly. Then Cloralinda saw that just beyond that pebble lay another, and then another, and still another. There was a long row of moon-bright pebbles in a straight line.

"Two children came into my forest once long ago when the trees were lower. They dropped these pebbles and the moonlight lit them so they could find their way home. The moonlight stayed in the pebbles, and they still light the path out of my forest. Follow them as far as they will take you. And when you are sure you are out of my forest, but *not* before, open the pouch and read the map. And finally, ask advice of those you meet and accept the help that is given you."

And before Cloralinda could say good-bye or thank you, the paws of Franz Lupus moved silently across the pine needles, and he was gone.

Chapter Four

PEBBLE BY PEBBLE, Cloralinda followed the path. And one by one, the pebbles grew dimmer as more light filtered through the trees, which were now shorter and farther apart. Before long, Cloralinda realized that the little pebbles were just ordinary small gray stones.

An owl flew alongside Cloralinda as she walked. "Would you like to hear a story?" it asked.

"Oh yes, please," said Cloralinda, for it was good to have company.

"Once upon a time there was a little princess. She was very pretty and very good. She went on a picnic with her aunt, and her crown fell off. Someone stole it. Do you want to know who, whoo, whooo?"

"Oh yes, please tell me!" said Cloralinda eagerly.

"I don't know who, whoo, whooo," said the owl. "I will tell you another story now. Once upon a time there was a tree. Someone chopped it down. Now would you like to know who, whoo, whooo?"

"Tell me about the princess and the picnic. Tell me about the aunt. Tell me who stole the crown," said Cloralinda.

"Oh, I only like the beginnings of stories," said the owl. "I cannot remember the middles, and sometimes the endings are sad. Now I will tell you another story. Long ago and far away, there were two tails. One was bushy . . . and one was *not!* There, wasn't that a good story?"

Cloralinda nodded sadly as she stared down at the pebbles. Ahead of her lay three more, and the third pebble was half hidden under a tall hedge.

"It is long past my bedtime," said the owl, for the sun was shining brightly. "I will tell you a bedtime story. Beware the woodchopper and his axe. That is who, whoo, whooo!" And the owl flew away.

When Cloralinda reached the high hedge where the last pebble disappeared, she saw that it was covered with thorns. The branches grew very thick, and she could see no way over or under it. Left and right, there were no more pebbles. The path had ended.

"I hope that I have come to the end of the forest of Franz Lupus," thought Cloralinda. "Now I can use that map to find my way to the princess."

Just then a small red fox with a bushy tail and a gold crown on its head walked over and peered curiously at her. He sniffed at her toes, and his whiskers and nose twitched. He walked around her three times, but he said not a word.

"Please, kind Mr. Fox, could you tell me a way to get over or under this hedge? I am Cloralinda, and I am taking this little golden ring to the princess." She showed the fox the little ring on her finger.

"Yip, yip," said the fox, and ran off a few yards.

"Do you understand me, Mr. Fox?" called Cloralinda, but the fox only began to chase its tail in circles, yipping gaily as it did so.

"Bears will grunt as bears do, owls will hoot, geese will honk, ducks will quack, and *foxes will yip*. I must be out of the forest of Franz Lupus. Yes, now I am sure I can open the pouch and read the map. Then I will find the safest and shortest route to the princess."

So Cloralinda eagerly untied the rope which tied up her tail. The little fox darted over and gave it a tweak with his sharp white teeth. Cloralinda hastily put her back to the hedge as she opened the pouch.

The map looked very old, ancient, in fact. It showed mountains, rivers, forests, towns, roads, and towers. One route was clearly marked with a sign that looked somewhat like an arrow and somewhat like an axe.

The route led directly to a palace marked with two flags.

Underneath the map, next to its legend, was lettered these words: THE ROYAL LAND OF EELOFF.

But poor Cloralinda! Just as she was studying the map, a strong gust of wind blew it from her hand. She ran stretching and leaping for it, but it was always just out of reach. It twirled over the tall hedge. Cloralinda fell into the hedge and scratched her hands and face on big thorns, but the map flew away.

Cloralinda called to Franz Lupus, but no answer came. Instead she heard someone singing in a high, squeaky voice:

> Three crowns there be,
> And one is for me!
> My name is Roy Ray,
> Fox King of the day.

There sat the little red fox with the small golden crown on his head. And he was talking! He had tricked her into thinking she was out of the forest of Franz Lupus by yipping when she met him. Too late Cloralinda remembered the warning the wolf had given her about an animal who would tweak her tail.

"If you will give me that ring, I will show you the way out of the forest. It is not far from here, but you will never find it without my help," said the fox with a wicked grin, his golden eyes twinkling.

"That I will never do," said Cloralinda. She made a fist of her left hand and shook it at the fox. "This ring belongs to the princess. I am supposed to take it to her, and take it to her I will. I will find my way out of the forest of Franz Lupus across, over, or under this bramble hedge."

Although Cloralinda spoke bravely, she felt quite the opposite inside.

> The crown of the princess of Eeloff
> Is mine and never will come off. . . .

sang Roy Ray the fox, and he pranced and danced away, his bushy tail sailing joyously behind him.

Cloralinda stood on tiptoe. She could not see over the hedge. What lay beyond she did not know. The rope and the pouch that had held the map of the land of Eeloff lay on the ground beside her as did the tip of her donkey tail. A goose flew over her head. "Please, what shall I do now?" called Cloralinda, remembering that Franz Lupus had told her to ask for advice.

"I'd follow my tail if I were you," called the goose.

Cloralinda's tail pointed right, and so to the right she turned and began to walk.

Chapter Five

To the right walked Cloralinda. High, dense and thorny, the hedge went on, as far as she could see. Cloralinda felt most discouraged.

Suddenly something tweaked at the tip of her tail. It was Roy Ray again.

"Now will you give me that golden ring in return for a way to get beyond this hedge?" he asked. He held the tip of Cloralinda's tail tight in his teeth.

Cloralinda did not answer him. She tugged at her poor tail, but the fox only held it tighter. He began to run and Cloralinda had to run with him. She had no choice. The gold crown of the princess of Eeloff glowed in the setting sun, gold as the foxy eyes that twinkled so wickedly.

They ran far and fast, but the hedge did not end, nor did it ever vary in height. The farther they ran, the more Cloralinda thought that perhaps she had come to the end of the world (if there was one).

But she never once considered giving the ring to the naughty fox, for as she said to herself, "I have left the cave which was my home, and I have come safely through the dark forest of Franz Lupus. And why? Only to give the ring back to the princess. So what would be the use of crossing the hedge without the ring? And yet, suppose I never cross the hedge, and stay here forever, neither here nor there!" Cloralinda was close to crying at this thought, but she *would not* let that fox see her cry. So she held in her tears, her eyes tight and dry.

On and on ran the fox, and on and on ran Cloralinda. Suddenly Cloralinda heard a surprising sound. She heard a dog bark. The friendly "Bow-wow" was a new and pleasing sound to Cloralinda. She was certain it came not from the forest of Franz Lupus but from the other side of the hedge. And Cloralinda knew then that there was a world beyond that hedge, and over that hedge she would go, somehow or other.

And just then, to her surprise, the fox let go of her tail. She had been running so fast that the sudden stop made her tumble to the ground, where she lay heaving to catch her breath.

"The hour between dog and wolf has come," said Roy Ray, "and that is the hour for me. Look at the sun, how he copies me, red and prancing, and full of fun! How his rays twinkle and sparkle, like my lovely shining whiskers! Good-bye, Cloralinda, and remember, one day that ring will be mine, and you will never get over the hedge!"

Roy Ray was gone. The sun tumbled low behind the hedge, and what the naughty little fox said seemed true. The sun did seem to mimic the grinning fox as Cloralinda lay on the damp ground, gazing at the tangled roots at the base of the hedge, and the deep moss, and the black earth.

Cloralinda heard the dog bark again. The sound was soft and faint, as though heard through fuzz and mist. Cloralinda frantically began to dig a hole under the hedge.

"A small hole is all I need . . . as small as I am. Yes, of course I can dig that small hole!" But the roots seemed to grow thicker, wider and stronger, the more she dug. The moon came up and gave good light, but all she could see were roots that seemed to have no end. Just when Cloralinda was sure she could dig no more, she felt something sharp and cold lying in the earth beneath the hedge roots. And by the bright moonlight she saw very clearly what it was.

In her hand Cloralinda held a tool that looked somewhat like an arrow and somewhat like an axe. Once before she had seen its likeness. On the map of the land of Eeloff, it had marked the path . . . the very map Franz Lupus had given her, the map she had been tricked into losing.

"Surely this axe will help me find the princess. For with an axe I can chop, and I can chop down this hedge. Oh, good Franz Lupus, you must have hidden this here for me! Thank you for helping me again."

And Cloralinda began to chop down the hedge.

Chapter Six

THE FULL, BRIGHT MOON gave Cloralinda plenty of light. She chopped away. The hedge stalks were thick, tough, and thorny, but the axe was unbelievably sharp. Cloralinda chopped and chopped and chopped. Hours passed and still she chopped stalk after stalk of the dense and thorny hedge, and made remarkably little progress. But strange to say, she grew neither sleepy nor discouraged, and her arms never ached, no matter how hard she chopped. She looked behind her and saw that she had cut a path more than twenty feet long, and still the hedge grew thick as ever before her.

Then, out of the darkest part of the forest, a huge shape appeared. Two red eyes glowed, and Cloralinda knew it was Franz Lupus. He kept his distance from her and watched, but he said not a word. For a long time he stood there, still as a statue, but for some reason, Cloralinda could not think of anything to say to him, and she felt afraid.

At last dawn crept along the bottom of the night sky, and just at that moment the last bush which formed the great hedge fell. Cloralinda had not even time to get a glance at the world she had opened up, for a woolly and chilling fog suddenly surrounded her. She heard from somewhere a rumbling, and a swishing of waves.

Nothing showed in the fog, not even the red eyes of Franz Lupus, not even the little golden ring that belonged to the princess. But Cloralinda could hear the big paws of Franz Lupus coming toward her. He stopped and let out a long and terrible howl. Cloralinda tried to say she was sorry, but he snarled and growled like the wolf he was.

"Go away, Cloralinda! You have cut down the walls of my forest. Now who knows who will enter it? You were a bad, bad girl to touch that axe. That woodchopper has caused me much trouble and woe. I myself buried his axe there many years ago. The owl warned you. Oh, what a bad girl you were to cut down my hedge! I might have helped you once more to find the land of Eeloff, but now you must go your way alone. Go away, and never, never come into my forest again. Oh, that axe! That terrible axe! And that fox—that tricky fox, what trouble he causes me!" Franz Lupus began to howl again, but not so fiercely this time. His howl was more like a long sob. Again and again Cloralinda told him how sorry she was, but the big wolf would not answer her.

Cloralinda could say no more. She tied up her donkey tail and picked up the axe and walked out into the foggy world beyond the forest. She seemed smothered in a cloud. She was cold and damp, and her dress, which had lasted so long in the cozy cave of the bears, was now full of tears and tatters.

She walked on and on through the fog. Suddenly she realized her feet were wet, and she thought she had stepped into a puddle. Then, to her alarm, she saw it was no puddle, but a wild river, and she quickly hopped backward to shore. The wind whipped up waves and wavelets, and icy drops blew off the water and drizzled into fog. Cloralinda looked down at the shining axe she held in her hand.

"If you were only a boat," she said sadly.

Now Cloralinda felt more discouraged than ever before. Here on this foggy shore there were no pine needles to keep her warm. The waves splashed and the wind roared, and she missed the great and lovely silence of the forest.

Then she heard the friendly barking that she had heard before. Coming toward her through the fog and mist was an old man. He stood in a strange-looking boat, which he poled toward shore, while a little hound stood barking eagerly in the bow. The old man wore a dismally ugly cape made of the skins of many small beasts. Woodchucks, raccoons, skunks and voles, mice and feathered birds and warty toads and slippery snakes were only a few of those whose skins Cloralinda recognized. Before he could reach the shore, his boat turned round and round in the whirlpools of the river.

"A very good morning to you, little lady," said the boatman, bowing low. "I hope you are well today. May I be of help to you?" Cloraldinda almost smiled, for the boatman was as polite in his manners as he was dismal in his appearance.

"Bow-wow! Arf-arf!" barked the dog, and he too sounded welcoming and pleasant.

"How do you do?" said Cloralinda.

The old man replied, "How do you do?"

Cloralinda said, "Very well, thank you," not because it was true, but to end the how-do-you-doing. The boat looked as if it might drift away.

"I cannot cross the river," called Cloralinda, and the boatman, with great difficulty, poled back to the shore. "My name is Cloralinda, and I seek the royal land of Eeloff. I come from the cave where the three bears live, beyond the great forest of the wolf, Franz Lupus. I have been cruelly tricked by Roy Ray, who says he is Fox King of the day. I have cut down the hedge of Franz Lupus with an axe I found, and he is very angry with me. I have lost my map, and I do not know where to go. For you see, I must find Eeloff and a certain princess."

The boatman took Cloraldinda's hand and helped her into the boat. But when he saw the axe he began to shake; he trembled so violently he had to sit down, and he shouted over and over again, "Where did you get this? Tell me, where did you find it?"

His fingers ran up and down the sharp and shiny edge, and he muttered things to himself that Cloralinda could not understand.

"I dug it up," the little girl answered when the old man had calmed down somewhat. "I found it over there, buried in the ground beneath the hedge,'' and she pointed backwards through the fog.

Just then a large wave splashed over the gunwales of the boat, which was really a gigantic dugout canoe made from an enormous tree. The bark, covered with moss and lichens, still grew on its sides. The old man's boat pole was a slender pine tree, with one cone still dangling sadly from a lone branch. The old man quickly put the axe between his teeth, grabbed his pole, and steered the boat out of the current.

With the axe still between his teeth he said, "Now I will tell you my story, long though it is, and full of woe. But first, my poor child, you are half frozen,'' and indeed, Cloralinda's teeth chattered, and she trembled all over. The old man put his cape around her shoulders, and it was so warm that it seemed less ugly.

"My name is Walter Whetstone,'' said the old man, as he pushed off from shore. "Once I was the head wood-chopper of the royal land of Eeloff. My good axe was given to me by the Egg Woman at the Mossy Well . . . my good axe. . . .'' and he took the axe from between his teeth, set it down gently beside him, and poled off into the wild waters.

Where she was going she did not know. She was

afraid, for she was leaving her forest, and the wood-chopper was a mysterious old man indeed. And what was it Franz Lupus had said of a woodchopper? And an axe? But Cloralinda was brave and as the boat dipped and rocked, she looked steadily ahead.

Chapter Seven

"First I will tell you something of the land of Eeloff," said Walter Whetstone. And Cloralinda listened eagerly.

"It is a good land in many ways. It is a famous land, for the people of Eeloff are very skilled in the manufacture of wooden toys. They make jack-in-the-boxes, toy trains and carriages, wind-up dragons that roar and birds that fly, mice that run on nearly invisible wheels, dolls and dishes and little castles with all their royal people, blocks, and boxes filled with smaller and smaller boxes. . . .

Oh, the toys of the land of Eeloff are wonderful indeed.

"And do you know why they are so far superior to any other wooden toys? It is because of the wood they are made from. It was my job, as head woodchopper, to cut this marvelous wood and bring it from a deep and dark forest to the land of Eeloff.

"I know little about the carving and turning of lathes, nothing of painting tiny faces and cutting little cogs and wheels and gears . . . that was the work of the others . . . but I do know woods! Hard, strong, clear-grained, I can tell good wood before the tree is cut.

"I believe I must have been born knowing good wood from bad, because when I was just a young boy, and that was very long ago, the Egg Woman at the Mossy Well gave me this axe. She said I was most fitted to be the head woodchopper of the land of Eeloff, and so I was. For many years I chopped down trees, and so wonderful was this good axe that I never needed to hone or sharpen it. In fact, it grew sharper with use. Although I grew older, my arms never became tired, and my muscles did not ache. I thank my good axe for that.

"One day I came to the finest tree I had ever seen. To me it was the tree of trees. I thought of the toys that could be made from that wood. How I longed to hear the ring of my axe against that good wood! How I longed to hear the magnificent crash and rumble as it fell onto the mossy ground!

"Now you may ask, why didn't I just cut it down, if my good axe was so sharp? No, it was not the axe that was a problem. It was the hole in the tree."

"What hole?" asked Cloralinda, for although the story made little sense to her, and it seemed as if Walter Whetstone were telling it to himself, she was eager to hear more.

"The dark hole, the deep hole, the hole by the roots. The hole where two red lights glowed, day and night, year in and year out."

Cloralinda drew in her breath. "Franz Lupus!" she murmured.

"No, it was not a human thing in there. It was the wicked monster of the forest. Wolf it may have been, but I have known wolves. There are good wolves and bad wolves, but this creature was a fiend, a monster. Many nights I heard it howl, and I declare, that was no ordinary howl, but some monstrous song—a spell, a chant, a charm. Something wicked sounded in that howl!

"I plotted and planned ways to lure that fiend out of the hole in my tree. I tempted those wicked eyes with the sight of fresh meat . . . fresh-killed porcupine and tender little rabbit, owl chicks just out of their nest, and dainty mice. But the fiend would have none of that. And then one day, something came my way that tempted the monster out of the hole. But first I must tell you about the king and queen and the little princess."

Cloralinda listened carefully. The water swirled around them and the wind blew, but she heard Walter Whetstone well.

"The king and queen of the land of Eeloff had grown old with no children. Even the Egg Woman at the Mossy Well and her magic medicines were no help.

"When everyone had given up hope, the king and queen had a little princess. Her name was Comet, a peculiar name for a princess, but it was whispered that this was a peculiar princess.

"In any case, there was someone who was not entirely happy that the little princess Comet had been born. That was her aunt, the king's younger sister. When the little princess Comet was born, the princess Mary Jane lost her chance to rule, and they appointed her royal nursemaid. And to tell the truth, I doubt that she would have ever made a good queen, for she was not a competent nursemaid. She had less sense than the baby princess.

"One day, the princess Mary Jane brought the baby princess Comet to my forest. Oh my, such fine food they brought for a picnic! I, who lived on berries, pine nuts, mushrooms, and baked squirrels, had never sniffed such delicacies. They brought honeycomb sandwiches on bee-dust bread, pickled plums, and hard-boiled robin's blue eggs. They got those from the Egg Woman at the Mossy Well. Magic eggs, I believe they were.

"And their clothes . . . not at all suitable for a picnic in the woods. The baby princess wore her little gold crown, easy to lose among the leaves. She wore a long white dress, not sensible for the thorns and brambles of the woods. Princess Mary Jane spread the tablecloth in a pretty clearing, and there they ate their lunch. Afterward, the princess Mary Jane sat down to read a book, and the little princess Comet crawled away into the woods. And then, oh my . . ."

Walter Whetstone sniffed a sob.

"What happened next?" Cloralinda asked and shook him.

"Oh, I have been punished. . . . How I have been punished!" cried Walter Whetstone, sobbing loudly by now. His dog howled in harmony with the old man's sobs.

"Oh, do get on with the story, please!" cried Cloralinda as she wiped the old woodchopper's tears away with a furry corner of the cape.

"It might never have happened, had I not wanted that tree so badly. I blame myself, but oh, I have been punished! The little princess crawled away, and along I came, merrily swinging my good axe and singing my favorite song. When I saw her crown flashing in the sunbeams, I ran toward her to pick her up, but then I saw something.

"The red-eyed monstrous fiend came out of the hole in the tree, my tree, the tree of my dreams, and trotted toward the baby princess. She smiled and cooed something. It grunted a bit and licked her, just for a taste, you know. Then that awful red-eyed beast picked up the little princess in its sharp teeth, and disappeared into the dark forest.

"Her crown fell off, but I did not even go to pick it up, for all I could think of was that the monster was out of the hole in *my* tree, and chop, chop, with my good axe I set to work!

"How did I know that I was loosening the powers of that fiend upon myself? I chopped my way through the great tree. My axe sparkled and chips flew and pine needles spun through the air. Then, just as the great tree was about to fall, a dreadful rush of water sounded from inside the tree. Suddenly I was drowning in a river. The water rose higher and higher, and whirlpools formed.

I lost my axe. Then the great tree fell over and floated away. I grabbed hold of it.

"I saw my dear dog Frisky, and I took him onto the tree. As we floated round and round, I heard a scream. There was the princess Mary Jane, splashing in the water. I took her on board the tree, and then mists covered us. Nasty-looking fish and spiny things poked their heads out of the water and showed their teeth.

"Although I had lost my good axe, I still wore a knife in my belt, and I made that tree of trees into a boat—this very boat that you are in. A small pine I had chopped down early that morning floated near, and became my boat pole. I poled for many days and nights, and all the while that silly Mary Jane was sobbing and carrying on, and calling for the baby princess. She didn't even call her by the right name.

"I told her the princess Comet was gone for good, either eaten by that fiendish wolf or drowned for sure, and all that she would say was 'Oh my big brother, what a bad girl your sister is! Oh my big brother, what will you do to me?'

"At last we came to a shore. It was a peaceful place, well cared for, and up the hill I saw a little house and a mossy well. I knew I had come home to the land of Eeloff. I poled carefully to shore and let the princess Mary Jane step off, and none too soon either, I can tell you that! Just as Frisky and I were about to disembark, a huge wave lifted my boat and pulled it out into the water.

"Many years have passed, I have grown old, and again and again I have tried to disembark in my homeland of Eeloff, but the same thing always happens. A giant wave always comes and washes me out into the river again. And now I know that I shall never come home to Eeloff, for this is my punishment.

"If I had followed the wolf and saved Princess Comet, none of these terrible things would have happened. I would be home now, in my pleasant house in the land of Eeloff. My fine axe would still hang on the wall. My good dog Frisky could sleep by the hearth, and I would live in peace. Instead, I am fated to go on poling my way back and forth (for I never give up trying to land) in this terrible river of my own making."

Terrible indeed was the tale the woodchopper told. Cloralinda was silent. She thought of the crown of the baby princess Comet that she had seen on the head of the naughty little fox. She thought of her friend, Franz Lupus, the great wolf, but then she shivered to think of that same red-eyed wolf and the baby princess who had crawled off into the dark woods.

And which princess did the ring belong to? The

baby or her nursemaid? And who was to say that Cloralinda too would not paddle forever in the great river made from the tree Walter Whetstone chopped down . . . the tree that had been home for Franz Lupus? Was that the punishment Franz Lupus had wished on her for cutting down his hedge? Cloralinda began to cry, and the old man joined her, and Frisky whimpered too.

Chapter Eight

SUDDENLY THE SUN BEAMED through the fog, and the gray mist disappeared. The river splashed gently onto a sandy beach. Green meadows spread out beyond the beach, and there was an old road, paved with cobblestones, that meandered up a gently sloping hill. At the top of the hill was a little house with a mossy well. And even before Walter Whetstone said a word, Cloralinda knew they had come to the shores of the land of Eeloff.

Walter Whetstone steered the boat near shore. Cloralinda stepped out onto the beach. Just as the old man was following her, a great wave came by and tossed the dugout into the river again.

As it floated backwards into the fog, Cloralinda called to him, "I have come through the dark forest of Franz Lupus, the red-eyed wolf, whom you called fiend and I called friend. I have seen the crown of the princess Comet on the head of that naughty fox, Roy Ray. I have discovered the axe that the Egg Woman at the Mossy Well gave you, and with that axe I have chopped down the hedge that hides the forest of Franz Lupus.

"Oh, Walter Whetstone, small as I am, if I have done these things, isn't it possible that I may help you to come home to the land of Eeloff? Perhaps the king and queen can help you. For now I must take them the ring that belongs to the princess. But which princess? Walter Whetstone, which princess wore a little gold ring?"

"I saw no ring," the old woodchopper called from deep in the fog. "Go to the Egg Woman at the Mossy Well. She will give you answers that are wiser than the king and queen. Not only is she wise, but she is most magical."

And then Cloralinda could hear him no more.

Chapter Nine

CLORALINDA CLIMBED THE HILL to the house by the mossy well. She knocked at the door and a kindly-faced, chubby old woman opened it.

"Are you the Egg Woman at the Mossy Well?" asked Cloralinda, although it was hardly necessary to inquire. On every shelf, in every corner, in all sizes and shapes of baskets and bowls, were all sizes, colors, and shapes of eggs. The Egg Woman assured Cloralinda that she was indeed herself and invited the little girl in to sit down. Best of all, she gave Cloralinda a delicious poached egg on raisin toast.

Then Cloralinda told her story. The Egg Woman listened with interest, and at last she said, "Let me see that ring."

Cloralinda gave the ring to the Egg Woman, who looked at it for a long time. Then she put it on a high and very dusty shelf.

"Please, Egg Woman, may I have the little ring?" asked Cloralinda, as politely as she could.

But the Egg Woman only chuckled and said, "Oh my goodness, no! What I find, I keep! Goodness, goodness . . . this ring is mine until you can find the princess Comet, and if you cannot find her, I do not know what will happen to Eeloff. It is totally, and I must say, *totally*, without leadership! I do my best, but magic will only serve so well. Good sense, kindness, wisdom, and leadership are needed too. Oh, especially good sense and kindness. They are always needed as much as magic. And now I must manage all alone with my magic, and I am getting tired."

She got up and began to rearrange baskets of eggs. "Such dust," she said wearily. "Dust and disorder."

Cloralinda had a thought. She had come far since she had kept the cave of the three bears so nice and tidy, but she knew she was still a good housekeeper. The Egg Woman's little house certainly did need dusting, and sweeping too. And perhaps, while cleaning the shelf, she could take the ring without being noticed.

"Please, Egg Woman, may I thank you for your hospitality by tidying your house?" asked Cloralinda.

"Oh my dear child, how kind of you to offer. Oh yes, I would like that," said the Egg Woman, and she handed Cloralinda a feather duster. Cloralinda worked away, but just as she reached up to the shelf with the ring, the Egg Woman grabbed the feather duster.

"No, no, no! Those are my silver spider eggs up there! Those hatch . . ." she bent down and whispered in Cloralinda's ear, ". . . *stars!*"

"No!" said Cloralinda. She thought the stars would be rather dim from dust when they hatched.

"How wonderfully tidy it all is," said the Egg Woman happily. "You are a kind and sensible child." She took a big, white egg with one gray feather stuck to it down from another shelf. It was all alone in a bowl, and the Egg Woman handled it very carefully.

"I will give you a little help in your search for the princess Comet. My magic cannot find her, for I have tried. But this is a very useful egg, and I have saved it for a special occasion. It was laid by Mother Goose herself. Whoever eats an omelet made from this egg cannot help but tell the truth. Use it wisely."

And with that advice the Egg Woman handed Cloralinda the white egg and shooed her on her way.

Chapter Ten

THE FULL MOON LIT HER WAY as she walked up the cobblestone road. Moonbeams shone on an old sign with the paint nearly worn off. Only the word *toys* still showed.

Cloralinda remembered what Walter Whetstone had told her of the wonderful toys made by the people of Eeloff. Could this be the toy factory? For when she looked beyond the faded sign she saw an old tumble-down brick building with many chimneys and tall glass windows, most of which were shattered. The distance to the old building was short, and Cloralinda walked quickly to a rickety old door and pushed it hard. It seemed to have been shut for many years, but, creaking and squeaking, the door opened just enough to let the little girl pass through.

Moonlight streamed in through the tall windows of shattered glass. Everywhere that Cloralinda looked, she could see long tables, and on those long tables there were rusty machines that worked no more. Wood shavings littered the floor and sawdust lay like yellow snow on everything. Broken bits of unfinished toys . . . arms of dolls, half-turned tops, trains without wheels, and round jack-in-the-box heads lay scattered around the floor and on the cluttered tables. The place seemed so abandoned that Cloralinda was startled to hear a soft song being hummed, a little like a lullaby.

There was another room, and Cloralinda entered it. Here open jars of paint stood on long tables. Around them lay paintbrushes with bright colors long dried in their bristles.

And in a dim corner a lady sat, humming a soft song as she stitched a suit for a wooden clown. On her head, Cloralinda saw a golden crown.

The lady let out a little shriek when she saw Cloralinda, but Cloralinda went up to her, curtsied, and said, "Your Majesty!" for she was sure this was the queen she sought.

But the lady said, "Get up little girl, and don't be so silly. I am no majesty. I am plain Mary Jane, and this is only a toy crown, like all the other toys in this factory. I work here. And there is no majesty, for the king and queen have taken off their golden crowns and gotten into their beds. They do not rule. Instead, they read stories and eat cookies, and cry for that which they lost long ago."

"And is that the princess Comet?" asked Cloralinda.

But the lady would not answer her. Cloralinda knew the time had come to use that magic egg.

She must make an omelet. She quickly gathered up a heap of wood shavings and sawdust. But she had no match to light the fire and no pan to cook an omelet in.

"Help me, Franz Lupus," she cried. "Please forgive me, and help me!"

Suddenly a window cracked. A small flaming meteor or star flew in through the cracked glass and landed. It landed on Cloralinda's pile of wood shavings and sawdust, and lit a fire. Flames soared up, and in those flames Cloralinda was sure she could see the two red eyes of

Franz Lupus, looking kindly at her. How far his magic traveled!

"Good Franz Lupus," whispered Cloralinda, "Now I know the princess Comet lives. Thank you."

Cloralinda found a wooden toy pan. And it must have been made of Walter Whetstone's finest wood, for it did not burn. The omelet smelled most delicious.

"Miss Mary Jane," said Cloralinda, "Please let me offer you this omelet. You look weak and hungry. I am sure that you have not eaten for days. Here, take a bite, and see how good it is." She picked up a toy spoon from a cluttered table and handed it to the lady. The omelet seemed to disappear in a trice.

"How good that was!" the lady said. "How hungry I was! And how lonely! For I have been here all along since the day I lost our baby princess in the forest. And that was many years ago. . . ."

Chapter Eleven

THE PRINCESS MARY JANE told a long tale, and it was
exactly like the one Walter Whetstone had told Cloralinda. Except for one thing.

After the princess Mary Jane had told Cloralinda
about the baby's disappearance, she said "I could never
be sure that I had lost the princess entirely by accident,
for there was always something about her that made me
ashamed."

"What do you mean?" asked Cloralinda.

"Oh, it was a terrible thing!"

"Please tell me," begged Cloralinda.

"Little girl, you must know this. All creatures are made as they should be, are they not?"

"I suppose so," replied Cloralinda. "But what was the terrible thing?"

"Horses have hooves, birds have wings, and fish and dragons have scales. And people have toes and fingers, and voices with which to speak. But little girls, especially princesses, *should not have donkey tails!*"

Cloralinda stood up tall and proud in front of the princess Mary Jane, untied her donkey tail, and said, "I am the long-lost princess Comet of the land of Eeloff."

And then Cloralinda fell down into a deep sleep, her donkey tail curled up around her.

PINK

Chapter Twelve

WHEN CLORALINDA AWOKE, it was morning. People surrounded her, and there was much whispering, staring, shoving, and jostling.

The king and queen got up out of bed, put on their crowns, and came to kiss their long-lost daughter. And to her surprise (although little surprised her now), as soon as Cloralinda stood up, the horrid old ugly cape turned into a lovely cloak of patchwork velvet, with gold threads holding the patches together.

The old queen put her own crown on Cloralinda's head, and the little girl knew that she had a great deal of work to do. She hugged and kissed her mother and father hello and then good-bye.

Then she and her aunt, Princess Mary Jane, walked away from the factory together, leaving behind the milling, chattering crowd.

They went first to see the Egg Woman at the Mossy Well, and the Egg Woman gave Cloralinda the little ring. As she already knew, it fitted her left hand perfectly.

"It was always tied around your neck when you were a baby," said Princess Mary Jane. "I had a hard time keeping you from swallowing it, you know." Then she looked down at Cloralinda's donkey tail.

"Excuse me, do you plan to, uh, let it, uh, hang down . . . your uh, uh, uh . . ."

"My tail?" said Cloralinda.

"Yes," replied Mary Jane, and she blushed and looked away.

"Of course," said Cloralinda. "It is by my tail I knew I was the princess. Not by the little gold ring, and certainly not by my name. And I believe it was my tail that made those wild beasts treat me well, for it made them feel I was one of them. So it probably saved my life.

You must learn to like it too. But tell me, why am I not called Comet?"

"That is my fault too," said Mary Jane. "The queen was especially partial to the name. She chose your name before you were born, and I myself was sure that had something to do with your being born with a tail, like a comet. So I hated it, and I called you Cloralinda. It means clean, and bright, and shining, like a star, but a star without a tail."

Cloralinda thought a moment.

Then she said, "I like both names so much that I think that when I am queen, I shall call myself Queen Cloralinda Comet."

And Cloralinda was so happy she skipped ahead of Mary Jane, who ran after her nervously, for she still felt afraid of losing the newfound princess.

Cloralinda skipped down to the peaceful sunny river. Only a fog bank toward the center hinted of poor Walter Whetstone. Cloralinda called him loudly, and after a while he came poling out of the mist, with Frisky barking merrily.

And the princess Comet stretched out her hand to Walter Whetstone, and to the old woodchopper's joy and amazement, no wave tipped up the dugout. He stepped ashore, and kneeled and kissed the ringed hand of the little girl who wore the golden crown and the velvet patchwork cloak.

"Thank you, Your Majesty," he said, bowing his head, but Cloralinda told him to look up at his old friend from the other side of the river. She told him that now Princess Comet was found, and the spell the wolf had cast was broken.

Walter Whetstone stood holding his boat pole in one hand and his good axe in the other. Just then a strong breeze came up and blew away the remaining pinecone from the pole. It landed in a field next to the Mossy Well, and on that field saplings began to sprout. Before their eyes, Cloralinda, Walter Whetstone, Mary Jane, and Frisky watched a dark forest grow.

More magic! Even the Egg Woman ran out of her little house and watched in wonder as the trees stretched higher and higher, and their branches wove together thicker and thicker.

Walter Whetstone ran like a young woodchopper into the forest. He sniffed the bark of those tall trees, and he shouted with joy. "What wood, what wonderful wood! It is the best I have ever seen. Oh, what toys this wood will make! What little cogs and wheels, what gears, what doll faces, what pots and pans, what castles, cars, carriages and blocks! Oh, what wood this is!"

Walter Whetstone did not hang his good axe over his fireplace. Once again, he was the head woodchopper of the land of Eeloff. Princess Mary Jane, with the help of Cloralinda, tidied up the factory and started all the machines running again. She much preferred making toys to being a royal princess.

One night, from far, far away, Cloralinda heard a long, sweet howl. She knew what she must do. She issued a proclamation to the workers in the toy factory to begin work on a beautiful, painted wooden statue of Franz Lupus. The Egg Woman contributed two red rubies from magic hummingbird eggs. Those were the eyes of the statue. The wooden body was covered with glowing silver leaf. There were silver and gold wire whiskers, and a painted pink tongue, and on the head of the statue Cloralinda Comet placed her father's golden crown, which he no longer wore.

On special holidays the statue was always paraded through the royal land of Eeloff, and there were those who said it brought good luck, although the Egg Woman at the Mossy Well disagreed. The luck was her magic, doing its usual good work, she said.

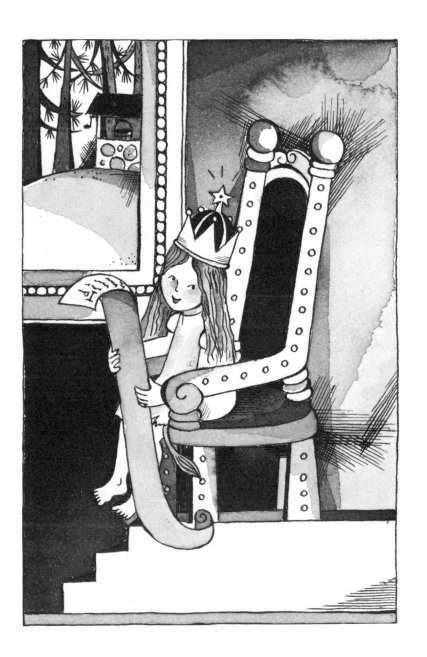

But Queen Cloralinda Comet did not trouble herself with wondering about these things. She was much too busy using kindness and good sense to run the kingdom.

ANNE ROCKWELL has written and illustrated many picture books. But *The Girl With A Donkey Tail* is her first long work of fiction. She said it was the most challenging project she has undertaken.

"Without a flow of pictures to carry the story, I had to develop the dialogue and description, keeping them in balance. Once the story was written, I thought the art would be easy. But I was surprised to find it so difficult! Each picture had to convey the mood and setting of the story, rather than illustrate a specific passage. The art required depth and a serious tone which is new to me.

"The idea of a donkey tail came to me when I was thinking about Erasmus' *Praise of Folly*. Folly is a lady or goddess with a donkey head. So Cloralinda had to be a bit of a donkey. A little tail seemed to suffice to 'donkify' her. She is foolish to leave the security of her bears' cave and to follow directions so literally, but she is very human in that when magic fails, she uses her head and discovers herself.''